THIS BOOK BELONGS TO:

_____

_____

_____

_____

_____

Written by Mary Bee
Illustrated by Jennifer Bartlett

This edition first published in 2020 by IG Design Group Americas, Inc.
©IG Design Group Americas, Inc., Atlanta, Georgia.

Published by IG Design Group Americas, Inc., Atlanta, GA 30342

Beautiful Sugar Ridge was not just any town. No, Sugar Ridge was a majestic town of sweets and treats. It had cake-pop trees and gumdrop hedges. It had houses made of cupcakes, gingerbread and chocolate wafers.

High above the streets of Sugar Ridge stood the icing-glazed ridge itself. At the foot of the ridge was an ice-cream castle, and through the center of town flowed Sugar Ridge's famous white chocolate river, smooth and delicious.

Today, Sugar Ridge was buzzing with excitement. The whole town was busy getting ready for its annual festival, the most exciting event of the year.

The Sugar Ridge Festival had rides, contests and games. This year's festival featured a Taffy Pull, Chocolate Dunk and Caramel Apple Dip.

CARAMEL DIP

The festival also had a Jelly Donut Fill. The donuts loved it because it tickled their bellies.

The cupcakes were especially excited about the Cupcake Walk. The winner of this year's contest would win the privilege of leading the Sugar Ridge Festival parade! Everyone was trying to predict who would be this year's best-decorated cupcake.

Most of the cupcakes had already made appointments with professional decorators and were deciding what kind of icing to wear for the contest. "I'm getting pink!" said Strawberry to the surprise of no one. "Probably with a strawberry."

"And I'm getting mint green with a ruffle around it," said Cocoa.

Carrot was getting a cream-cheese star, and Red Velvet was getting minidollops in a lovely pastel-red buttercream.

The cupcakes turned to Vanilla. "What are you getting?"

"I'm not 'getting' anything. I'm doing my own."

"Your own?" they questioned in disbelief. "You're doing your own?"

"Yes," answered Vanilla. "I'm doing my own."

"Well, it probably won't look very good," said Strawberry. "What kind of icing are you going to do?"

"I don't know—maybe confectioners' sugar, butter and milk."

"What color?" Cocoa wanted to know.

"I think I'll do white," she said.

"White?" they exclaimed, shocked. "No way! You've got to be kidding!"

"Why not?" responded Vanilla. "I like white."

"But it's so plain and boring," said Strawberry.

Now Vanilla was all the more determined to create decorations that would surprise them. "I'll show everyone that vanilla doesn't have to be plain or boring!" she said to herself.

She began collecting all of the ingredients she needed at the grocery store: confectioners' sugar, vanilla extract, butter, milk and food coloring.

On the morning of the festival, Vanilla carefully mixed and spread the icing. It went on beautifully, and she was very satisfied with the results. Still, it was a little, well, vanilla, she thought. Perhaps it did need a little something. But what?

"You look beautiful," said Vanilla's mother.

"Thanks, Mom," replied Vanilla. "But I'm not quite finished yet."

"No? What are you going to do?"

"I'm not sure yet," said Vanilla. "Maybe just a little swirl of yellow."

So Vanilla took a little bit of the remaining white icing and put it into a smaller bowl. She added some yellow coloring and worked it into the icing. Then she applied a little swirl of yellow over the white. It was nice, she thought, but it needed something more. A little swirl of green might be nice.

Again Vanilla colored a bit of the white icing. This time she created a green swirl next to the yellow one. *Ooh, that's really pretty!* she thought.

Now Vanilla was really excited, but she wasn't finished yet. She had an idea. She created a blue swirl next to the green and purple next to the blue. Next she added a swirl of red. Then she finished with a swirl of orange between the red and yellow. Now Vanilla's white topping became a beautiful rainbow swirl! It might not be professionally done, she thought, but it certainly made her happy! It made Vanilla's mom happy too. "Why, Vanilla, I'm so proud of you! That's just lovely!"

The festival was a thrilling and colorful sight, with taffy-striped tents, colorful flags and balloons. There were so many exciting things to do! Vanilla's first stop was the Chocolate Dunk. There was a peanut sitting in the dunking booth, a contraption with a moving seat suspended over a large tub of chocolate. Participants threw a ball at the target that, when triggered, suddenly lowered the seat, dunking the peanut into the chocolate. The peanut seemed to enjoy the whole process, and Vanilla thought he looked more and more handsome with each dip.

It was fun to watch the Chocolate Dunk, but Vanilla needed to hurry on to the location for the Cupcake Walk. As the contestants arrived for the contest, all eyes were on Vanilla.

The other cupcakes weren't quite sure what to think. No one had ever considered using multiple colors. It just wasn't done. And though Vanilla's work wasn't professionally done, it was rather pretty, the others thought. It made them just a little nervous. But surely the judges would prefer a professional job.

The stern-looking judges—a donut, an ice-cream cone and a chocolate bar—sat ready with their glasses down on their noses, their official contest clipboards in front of them. Then Mint Chip walked slowly across the stage while the judges scrutinized, writing busily on their clipboards.

JUDGES PANEL

"Vanilla," whispered Strawberry, "your colorful icing is really pretty. You did a nice job!"

"Thanks," replied Vanilla. "And your strawberry is just beautiful!"

Finally the moment they had been waiting for arrived.

The contest official stepped forward and spoke: "First of all, our judges would like to say that all of your decorations are beautiful. It was most difficult to make a decision. The winner, however, was chosen not only for the appeal of their decor but the novelty as well."

Vanilla drew in her breath.

"The winner of this year's Cupcake Walk is Vanilla with her rainbow-swirl icing!"

Vanilla blushed at the judges' approving nods and the audience's rousing applause; she couldn't believe that she had actually won.

The other contestants looked on admiringly as she stepped forward to shake hands with the official. It was more exciting than she had ever imagined.

"Tell us, Vanilla, who did your icing?" asked the official.

"Why, I did," said Vanilla. "It's more fun to do your own!"

There was a murmur from the crowd, then many oohs and aahs! This, too, was something new. No one had ever before done their own decorating!

So the next day, Vanilla, with her rainbow swirl, led the beautiful Sugar Ridge Festival parade. The other cupcakes marched proudly behind her, followed by the cookies, popsicles, lollipops, donuts and a few little gumdrops scattered all around.

"I'm going to wear rainbow swirl next year," said Strawberry to Cocoa.

"But you can't," said Cocoa. "I'm sure Vanilla will want to wear rainbow swirl. She invented it!"

"No," said Vanilla. "Anyone can have rainbow swirl. Next year I'm going to create something different!"

THE END